The Sock Monkey
Night Before Christmas

Larisa Lambert Mills

The Sock Monkey Night Before Christmas

Copyright © 2013 Sweetwater Press

ISBN:9781468283549

Illustrations by Michael Rogalski

Printed in China

The Sock Monkey
Night Before Christmas

by

Larisa Lambert Mills

SWEET
WATER
PRESS

'Twas the night before Christmas,

when all through the house

Not a creature was stirring, not even a mouse.

The socks were all hung by the chimney with care,

In hopes that Saint Nicholas soon would be there.

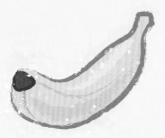

The sock monkey children were snug in their beds,

While candied bananas danced in their heads.

And mamma and I in our tufted knit caps,

Had just settled our brains for a long winter's nap.

When in the backyard there arose such a clatter,

I popped from my bed to see what was the matter.

Close to the window my nose I did press,

Wondering if I might see a big mess!

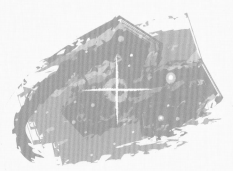

The man in the moon, he smiled down on the snow,

And shone bright as day on the scene down below.

When, what to my black button eyes should appear,

But a miniature sleigh, pulled by eight sock reindeer.

With a little toy driver, so happy and thick,

I knew in a moment it must be Saint Nick.

Faster and higher than the wind they did fly,

Santa called and the reindeer slipped through the sky!

Now Zigzag! Now, Stripe! On Tinsel! On Holly!

On Buttons! On Ribbons! On Silver! On Jolly!

To the top of the porch! To the top of the Wall!

Now dash away! Dash away! Dash away all!

As snow flakes are falling, and moved by the wind,

Saint Nick and the toys, the Christmas spirit did send.

So up to the house-top, the gift-bearers flew,

Pulling a red and gold sleigh—all shiny and new.

And then, in a twinkling, I heard on the roof

The padded, soft landing I knew was my proof

That Sock Monkey Santa and friends had come 'round

To bring to us all the season's best they had found.

He was dressed all in knit, from head to his feet,

And his big, red-lipped smile welcomed all he did meet.

A bundle of gifts he had on his back,

So full of surprise, like a Box hiding Jack.

His eyes, how they shone! His face was so merry!

His ears were like flaps, his mouth red as a cherry!

His smile was so wide that it cast quite a glow,

And the end of his tail looked like cream-colored snow.

His knit was soft brown, all mottled but neat,

With cream-colored ends on his hands, tail and feet.

He had a broad smile and a long tail like a tube,

That swung as he hopped and showed his good mood.

His seams, they were popping, his stuffing spilled over,

With surprise I looked on—my mouth I did cover.

A swing of his foot and a wave of his arm,

Let me know right away he was chock full of charm.

He spoke not a word, but went straight to his work,

Arranging the gifts, then he turned with a jerk.

He laughed as he straightened the tree that he bumped,

And giving a nod, up the chimney he jumped!

Sock Monkey Santa and his team, they all whistled,

And away they did fly like the down of a thistle.

And I heard them sing out, as they drove out of sight,

Happy Sock Monkey Christmas! And to all a good night!

The End